A CRAVING FOR CARVINGS

A Century Cottage Cozy Mysteries short story

DIANNE ASCROFT

Lois Stone turned the page of the novel and glanced up, casting her gaze from M.M. Kaye's *The Far Pavilions* to the uneven sidewalk in front of her house then back to the book. The mature maple tree on her lawn partially shaded her from the sunbeams dappling her veranda with late morning light. A soft breeze kept the mounting August heat at bay. She had known the moment she first saw the house that this veranda was somewhere she could relax, and now that she was settled into her new home, she was glad to finally do so.

And she was going to finish reading this book. She hadn't had the heart to read it after her husband James left it unfinished three years ago when he was mugged in their local park and the shock caused his fatal heart attack. He had intended to pass the book on to her after he read it, but after his untimely death she had put it back on the bookshelf and had only noticed it again as she unpacked in her new house. When she finally began reading the book earlier this month, the theft of an antique watch had altered her plans again. Rather than reading, she spent a frantic week working with her friend Marge to find the watch so that it could be presented to the local museum during Fenwater's sesquicentennial celebration.

Lois had moved from Toronto to Fenwater to enjoy the tranquillity of small-town life. Since she had spent the past month unpacking, settling into her new home and chasing a thief, she was sure that she now deserved a quiet Saturday morning with her book, sampling that tranquillity in a Muskoka chair on her front veranda.

"Hello, lovely morning, isn't it?"

Lois looked up from her book. An older man with grey hair and a neatly trimmed beard was standing on the sidewalk in front of her house. She recognised his face as they had exchanged greetings several times when they passed each other on the street.

"It sure is."

"Since I've seen you around here a few times lately, I thought you must live in the neighbourhood," the man continued.

"Yes, I moved into this house about a month ago."

"You were smart to snap up one of our century houses. The grey granite stonework is magnificent and they were built to last."

"I know. I fell in love with it the moment I saw it. I'm a real history buff so it's amazing to own one of these old houses. If only the walls could tell us what they've seen during the past century."

The man nodded his agreement. "Yeah, wouldn't that be something? By the way, I'm Greg Wend. I live at the end of this block." He gestured away from the town's main street.

"Nice to meet you. I'm Lois Stone."

"I'm sure we'll soon get to know each other. Folks are friendly on this street." Greg smiled, glancing down the street then back at her. "Well, I should head into town and get a few things. Are you coming to the Fenwater Flavours Festival at the market this afternoon?"

Lois shook her head. "No, I usually love things like that. But I've had a busy month and I'm treating myself to a day at home."

"Well, you'll be sorry you missed it. If you have a sweet tooth, there's some real temptations." Greg laughed and patted his slightly padded waistline. "I have no willpower – I always come home with a full shopping bag. I'm a terrible grouch without something to keep me sweet. That's my excuse anyway."

Lois chuckled. She couldn't imagine Greg in a bad mood. He seemed such a pleasant man. "It sounds wonderful but, like I said, I'm not moving from this veranda today. I'll be there next year."

"Well, don't say I didn't warn you what you're missing. Now I better go and get my errands done so I can enjoy the afternoon at the festival. See you again." Greg raised his hand in farewell as he walked away.

Lois smiled to herself as she returned to her book. One of the reasons she had chosen to sit on the front veranda instead of retreating to the shaded backyard was to have a chance to meet her neighbours. She had chatted with Sally and Joe, the nice young couple across the street, a couple of times but she didn't even know their surname and, except for the families that flanked her house, she hadn't met any of her other neighbours. If she wanted to become part of the community, she needed to make the effort to meet people. She wasn't as outgoing as her friend Marge, so this seemed like a nice way to break the ice.

Three-quarters of an hour later, the sound of a dog whining made Lois raise her head from the novel again. She glanced first at her calico cat stretched out beside her chair on the wide wooden planks of the veranda. The cat's eyes were closed and her body relaxed – only a slight movement of her ears indicated that she had heard the dog. Obviously Ribbons didn't find it threatening. She was glad that her other calico cat, Raggs, was asleep upstairs in the bedroom; dogs terrified her.

Lois turned her attention to the sidewalk, where a middle-aged woman, wearing knee-length navy shorts and a floral-patterned cotton blouse, tugged at the leash attached to a stocky West Highland white terrier, trying to counter the dog's lunges toward Lois's veranda.

The woman smiled apologetically. "Don't worry. He just wants to say hello. He doesn't chase cats. He actually likes them."

"That's good to know though I'm not worried. Ribbons can take care of herself, I've found."

"That's a good thing. I can't let Snowy out of my sight – who knows what mischief he'd get up to." Giving the leash a sharp tug, the woman glanced down at the dog. "Stop that now, Snowy, and behave." She turned back to Lois. "I'm Connie Harris. I live across the street, a few doors down. I'd noticed you'd moved in and meant to drop by before now."

"It's nice to meet you. I'm Lois Stone." Lois nodded to the cat. "And that's Ribbons. Her sister, Raggs, is inside."

As Lois spoke, she noticed Greg Wend coming toward them from the direction of the town, bags gripped in both hands. He managed to raise one hand in salute, nodding to each of the women as he passed. "Hello, ladies."

The women returned his greeting then Connie turned back to Lois. "Your cat's gorgeous. Her white coat looks like an artist dabbed it with dots of magnificent colour."

"Thanks." Before Lois could compliment Snowy in return, the dog tugged vigorously at its leash again, nearly unbalancing Connie.

"I better get going." Connie inclined her head toward the dog. "I need to tire him out this morning so he'll behave while I'm at the Fenwater Flavours Festival this afternoon. See you there."

Before Lois could explain that she wasn't going to the festival, the dog yanked Connie away from her. Lois chuckled as she returned to her book. She was glad that cats didn't need to be walked. She loved walking but enduring a wrestling match with an animal at the end of a leash every time she went out didn't appeal to her.

Lois slipped into her book again and lost track of time. She was dimly aware of one or two people passing the house, but she didn't look up despite her intention to meet her neighbours. The sound of the telephone ringing inside the house finally roused her. She tilted her ear toward the screen door and listened, hoping that whoever it was would give up. But the telephone kept ringing and she reluctantly decided she had better answer it before the disturbance to the drowsy morning stillness annoyed her neighbours.

As she set her book facedown on a small wooden table, painted forest-green to match her chair, and stood up, a heavyset man, wearing an orange-checked shirt and beige shorts, strode past. She didn't remember ever seeing him around the neighbourhood before. When their gazes met, the man quickly looked away, ignoring her as he hurried along the street. Lois raised an eyebrow as she watched him. *Goodness gracious, what an unfriendly man.*

The telephone's insistent ringing drew her attention again and she slipped into the house to answer it.

"Hi, Marge!"

"How did you know it was me?" the loud voice at the other end of the line spluttered.

"Most people would've given up after the first few rings."

Marge laughed. "But I know how long it takes to pull you out of a good book. Is two o'clock okay to meet at the market?"

Lois's brow wrinkled. "We didn't make plans to meet today, Marge. I've got a date with my book on the veranda."

"But you've got to come to the Fenwater Flavours Festival. You need to check out the competition if you're gonna be the 1984 champion with your banana and raspberry muffins."

"Let's worry about next year later. I need a break after all the worry we had over that stolen watch a couple weeks ago."

"Yeah, I guess we both do." Marge paused and her voice took on a conspiratorial tone. "But I overheard Bruce Murray telling the cashier in the hardware store this morning that he's going. I'm sure he'd be glad to see you."

"I can see him any time and we're just friends, that's all," Lois said quickly.

She was glad Marge couldn't see her face redden as she thought of the carpenter's warm brown eyes and the way he brushed his sandy hair from his forehead as he chatted with her. They were a good team when he had helped her and Marge catch that watch thief. And he had dropped by her house for coffee a couple times since then when he was in the neighbourhood. But, despite Marge's overactive imagination, he was just a friend. She hadn't even considered dating since James died.

"Well, I could use company," Marge wheedled. "I don't fancy going on my own and it's too much walking for my mom."

Lois shook her head, smiling to herself. She was sure her gregarious friend could easily mingle at any social event on her own. Marge knew nearly everyone in town and didn't need anyone to lean on. Lois easily saw through Marge's excuse: her friend was giving her a chance to meet people. The two women had been friends for years and Marge had been her rock after James died. So, no matter how much she wanted to stay at home today, she couldn't rebuff Marge's attempt to help her.

Lois took a deep breath. "Okay, two o'clock sounds good. I'll see you at the market."

2

Lois sighed with relief as she stepped into the cool market building, glad to be out of the sun's glare. The warm morning had honoured its promise to become a scorching afternoon. She felt clammy even though the walk from her house was a short one, just two blocks from the far end of the main street. She stopped inside the entrance to compose herself, her eyes widening as she noted the market's transformation since she had last been there. Multi-coloured streamers, balloons and a Flavours Festival banner hung from the walls and ceiling. Folding tables had been set up end-to-end to form a long table along one wall and draped with crisp, white tablecloths. Pies, cakes, muffins, and cookies were heaped on plates and cake stands along the length of the makeshift table. Lois's mouth began to water as she eyed the tempting array of goodies.

A hand gripped Lois's shoulder and a familiar voice whispered in her ear. "Don't worry. None of these can compete with your baking."

She grinned at Marge. "I don't know about that. They do look yummy. I should really resist but, in case I enter next year's competition, I better sample a few – just to compare, of course."

Marge laughed. "Good. You'll be my excuse for indulging today. You need my opinion. Come on, I'll introduce you to the bakers."

"Okay – as long as you don't start praising my baking to them. I'd die of embarrassment if you did."

"Don't worry. When have I ever embarrassed you?"

Lois could think of a few incidents off the top of her head, but refrained from mentioning any of them. Marge led her along the table, chatting with the bakers standing behind their creations. Lois recognised several of the women as members of the local library where she had recently begun working part-time. She knew she'd never remember the names of all the women she met, but she would recognise their faces when she next saw them and would be able to say hello. As they worked their way along the table, Lois bought a spiced apple rum cake from one baker, and half a dozen colourfully iced gingerbread men from another who had a blue ribbon prominently displayed beside her goods.

If I bump into Bruce today maybe I'll invite him over for a slice of the cake, Lois thought. *It wouldn't mean anything. I just shouldn't eat a whole cake on my own.*

Marge broke into her thoughts. "It's too bad we missed the judging but at least we got here before everything sold out."

"Yeah, I wouldn't have wanted to miss that spiced apple rum cake." Lois glanced away from the baked goods table to an aisle which ran at right angles to it. A couple weeks ago she had noticed a lovely handstitched burgundy quilt on a stall at the far end of the aisle that would be perfect on her bed. She took a step away from Marge. "I'm just going to have another look at that quilt I told you about. Won't be a minute."

As she started up the aisle someone stepped into her path. She glanced up to find a pair of warm brown eyes looking at her. She tried to keep her tone of voice casual as she greeted their owner. "Oh, hi, Bruce."

"Hi, Lois. I wasn't sure if I'd run into you here – you certainly don't need to buy any of these goodies. But since I don't have your baking skills, I'm stocking up." Bruce chuckled as he held up a bag filled with baked goods.

Lois felt the heat rising to her face at Bruce's compliment and hoped he wouldn't notice how he had managed to fluster her. "Well, I couldn't resist a spiced apple rum cake. It looked delicious." She hesitated then pushed herself to speak. It was just an invitation to drop by for coffee and a chat after all. "Why don't you drop over when you've got time and sample it?"

"Mmm, sounds good. I will, thanks. But I know it won't be as good as anything that comes out of your oven."

Even though she had no doubt that Bruce was just being kind, his praise and his admiring gaze felt good. A smile lit up her face. "I'm just popping over to have a look at something on one of the stalls. I'll be back in a jiffy."

Before she could move, she heard a man's urgent voice behind them. "Bruce – I guess you haven't heard about Greg?"

Bruce turned to face the man. "No, what?"

"He's been taken to hospital."

Bruce frowned. "Oh, dear. What's wrong?"

"Someone attacked him. I saw the ambulance outside his house when I was on my way here and stopped to speak to him for a minute when they brought him out."

"Is he badly hurt?"

"I don't think so. He got hit on the head and doesn't

know how long he was knocked out. When he came round, he managed to phone for help."

Bruce turned to Lois. "That's close to where you live – the end of your street."

Lois narrowed her eyes as she looked at the man who had brought the news. "Did you say Greg? That isn't Greg Wend, is it?"

"Yeah, do you know him?"

"Not well, but we introduced ourselves this morning when he passed my house. He seemed nice. Why would someone do such a thing to him?"

"I don't know. I can't think of anyone who'd want to hurt him." Bruce turned from the man to Lois. "Sorry, I haven't introduced you. This is Norm Henderson." He then turned to the man to introduce Lois to him.

Norm replied to her question. "He surprised a burglar and the burglar panicked and hit him."

Lois shivered at the mention of a burglary so close to her house. She knew crime was rare in the town but, as a result of her efforts to catch the thief who stole the antique watch earlier in the month, her home had been broken into twice. The last thing she wanted to hear was that there had been another burglary on her street. Lois frowned as she thought about what Norm had said. "The burglar panicked – how do you know that?"

Norm hesitated. "Uh, I don't know." He shrugged. "But Greg's a nice guy. I can't see anyone wanting to hurt him, I guess."

"I wonder if he saw the burglar?"

"No, he was hit from behind. He never turned around."

When Lois raised her eyebrows questioningly, Norm indicated the back of his head with his hand. "That must be what happened – the gash is there."

Lois nodded. Out of the corner of her eye she saw

Marge hurrying toward them. Behind her friend she caught a glimpse of an orange-checked shirt and recognised the unfriendly man she had seen walking past her house earlier. Avoiding eye contact with the bakers standing behind their goods, the man moved along the table, his gaze fixed on the confectioneries.

What an odd man. He certainly isn't very sociable but he must like sweet treats enough to endure coming into the busy market. I must remember to point him out to Marge and ask if she knows him, Lois thought.

When Marge was still several feet from Lois, she shouted, "You'll never believe it! An Indian carving was stolen in a burglary on your street. Good thing you don't have anything that valuable in your house."

Lois merely nodded, her lips pursed, as Marge stopped beside her. She didn't really like having her personal information thrown out for everyone to hear but in this case it might be a good thing if people knew she didn't have anything worth stealing. She didn't want to experience another break-in. And she wasn't surprised that, even though Marge hadn't been there, she had the full story already. Her friend had a nose for news.

"Norm just told us about the burglary too. How do you know what was stolen?" Lois asked.

"As they were putting him in the ambulance, Connie Harris heard Greg telling a police officer that before he got clobbered he had noticed his Haida Indian bowl was gone. He was really upset about it."

Lois glanced at Norm. His gaze was fixed on the floor, his brow drawn down in a deep frown. Lois thought she heard him mutter something about how Greg never missed anything.

Lois rubbed her hand across the back of her neck. "I

know original Indian art is valuable but one bowl couldn't be worth stealing, could it?"

Bruce raised his eyebrows and nodded slightly. "I saw the bowl when I did some carpentry work at Greg's house. It's beautiful – carved into the shape of a beaver, the Haida symbol for determination and hard work, and it's more than a hundred years old. It's made from argillite – a kind of slate the Haida Indians quarry at a secret location on Queen Charlotte Island in B.C. Its composition is different than any other argillite, and only the Haida Indians carve with it. The things they make from it can sell for several hundred dollars."

"Wow! How do you know so much about it?" Lois asked.

"I like Native art and I've made a few display pedestals and cabinets for art collectors. Several local people I know collect Haida art. There's a few of those argillite bowls kicking around town. What a shame that Greg's was stolen. It's his pride and joy."

"Well, hopefully he wasn't badly hurt in the burglary. Even a valuable bowl can always be replaced," Lois replied.

After murmurs of agreement, silence descended on the group. Lois thought it might be a good time to slip away to have a look at the quilt but as she took a step back from the group, Dave Stewart joined them.

The market stall owner was dressed in the red Stewart kilt that he always wore for civic festivities. "I heard something just now about Greg Wend getting burgled."

"Yeah, Marge just told us he had a Haida bowl stolen from his house," Bruce replied.

Dave's eyes widened. "Now that's quite a coincidence. I had a Haida bowl – a salmon design, one of the fertility ones – on my stall." Dave nodded in the direction of the aisle where his stall was. "I know it was there when I opened 'cause I dusted in that display cabinet this morning, but a little while ago I noticed it was gone."

"Was the cabinet locked, Dave?" Lois asked.

Since moving to Fenwater, Lois had marvelled at how trusting people in the town were compared to city folk. Locks didn't seem to be considered a necessity here.

Dave shook his head. "No, I was around most of the morning. I only popped out for half an hour. I meet Roy Lowry, the jeweller, at the Honey Pot for coffee on Saturday mornings. Rita at the next stall watches mine while I'm away. I've never had any problems before."

"Is anything else missing?" Lois asked.

"I've had a look through my stock but nothing jumps out at me. I think everything else is there."

Lois remembered the eclectic array of antiques on tables, in display cabinets and scattered on the floor in Dave's stall. It might take him a while to be certain whether anything else was gone. "Have you reported the theft?"

"No. I wasn't sure if I'd been robbed. But if Greg has had one stolen today then mine must've been too." Dave frowned. "I wonder why someone wants those bowls? I've got other items in my stall that are as valuable. Sometimes people are odd." He shook his head. "Well, I saw a police constable patrolling the far aisle a few minutes ago. I guess I'd better find him and report the theft. See you folks later."

As Dave walked away, Marge glanced around the group. Each of them, except Norm Henderson, was clutching a shopping bag. "Well, I think we're all stocked up on goodies and there's nothing we can do to help Greg right now, so why don't we head over to the Honey Pot? Since the festival is on, they might let us sample our purchases with our coffees." Marge lowered her voice and spoke into Lois's ear. "Unless you've made other plans?"

Lois felt her face flush as she shook her head. She said quickly, "The Honey Pot sounds good."

"Count me in," Bruce said.

"Thanks for the invitation," Norm said. "But I just got here so I'll stick around and do a bit of shopping."

Marge called over her shoulder as she strode down the aisle, "Right, folks. All those who need coffee, follow me."

Lois and Bruce fell in behind Marge as she cut a path through the crowd to the market entrance.

3

"You keep that spiced apple rum cake for later." Marge angled a grin at Lois when Bruce wasn't looking. "I'll share out some of these banana muffins and cinnamon cookies. I bought loads."

The waitress set their cups of coffee on the table. With a wink, Marge handed her two cinnamon cookies. "These are for your coffee break. You never saw these other ones on the table."

"Thanks! I never say no to cookies." The waitress grinned. "And, you know what? You're right. I never saw a thing."

Marge returned the waitress's grin then turned back to Lois and Bruce seated across the booth from her. "Okay, so what's going on? Why the sudden interest in Haida bowls? I thought totem poles were the most popular Indian artworks."

"They are," Bruce replied. "Even the small ones often sell for more than the bowls."

"So why does a thief want bowls then?" Lois asked.

"Yeah, I don't get it," Marge echoed.

Bruce drew his eyebrows together and stared at the table. "I didn't either at first but I think I see now. Not bowls – a bowl." He raised his head to look at the women. "I know of one bowl around here that's worth a lot more than the ones that were stolen."

"Oh – I never had you pegged as an art expert," Marge said between bites of a banana muffin.

"I'm not. But I meet collectors through my furniture carving and I hear things. There was a lot of talk a couple months ago about someone who had bought a very rare Haida grease bowl carved in the shape of an animal with a human head at an auction in Toronto. It was made around the beginning of the 1800s – which means it's nearly twice as old as the two bowls that have been stolen."

"Well, it would obviously be of historic interest," Lois said. "But is it worth much more than the others?"

Bruce nodded emphatically. "Oh, yeah, it is. The ones that were stolen are worth a few hundred dollars each. That one's worth at least fifteen thousand dollars. Maybe more if it went to auction again."

"Wow!" Marge exclaimed. "Someone better tell whoever has it to put it under lock and key until the thief is caught."

"That's the thing though – it was bought anonymously. It's rumoured to have been bought by someone in town but no one knows who."

"So you think the thief might be looking for it then?" Lois asked.

"I'd bet on it," Bruce replied.

"If that's the case, I may know how we can catch him," Lois said slowly.

Bruce narrowed his eyes as he regarded Lois. "After all the hassle over that watch, I thought you were going to leave crime-solving to the police in future."

"I am." Lois pursed her lips and glanced down at the table. "But I don't like to think of that nice man, Greg Wend, being attacked. And Dave Stewart helped us stop that other thief from getting away with the watch. We can repay him by helping to find these bowls. After all, one of them is his." Lois rubbed the back of her neck as she tried to gather her courage. She knew Bruce wouldn't like this. "But I doubt the police would approve of my plan. I think it would work though so maybe we should give it a shot."

Marge's eyes were dancing. "Go on, tell us what you have in mind."

"Well, if Bruce could put the rumour around that I bought the rare grease bowl and it's at my house then we might lure the thief to come after it."

"Good plan but let's say it's at my house, not yours," Bruce said.

"No, it should be my house. It's not far from where the other robberies happened so that should make the thief feel confident. And people don't know much about me yet so they won't know whether I might have any valuable art. Besides, as a woman on my own, I'll seem an easier target than you."

Bruce nodded reluctantly. "Okay, I can see those are good points. I'll put the rumour around and we'll see if anyone bites." He focused an intense gaze on Lois. "But I'm going to insist that I stay at your house until we catch the thief."

He didn't notice Marge's grin or the wink she directed at Lois.

❧ 4 ❧

Lois tiptoed into the living room and left the door to the hall open behind her, moving cautiously in the dark. "I've turned off the light in my bedroom as if I've turned in for the night and closed the cats in the room. They'll sprawl on the bed and conk out. How many nights do you think this might take, Bruce?"

"I put out the rumour to a few people early this morning. I let it slip that it's in the sideboard in your dining room so we'll know where he'll be headed. I'd say word will spread fast and the thief won't waste time. If he's heard, he'll probably be here tonight."

"Well, that's a good thing. I don't fancy being the third wheel for nights on end, even if Lois promises to keep making tasty suppers for us," Marge said with a chuckle. "The chicken cacciatore tonight was delicious. I really shouldn't have had the spiced apple rum cake too."

"Oh, Marge, cut it out. You're not a third wheel. The three of us are a team." Lois was glad no one could see her blushing. She quickly changed the subject. "Oh, I meant to tell you – I saw this strange man earlier. He had an orange-checked shirt and avoided looking at or speaking with anyone. He walked past my house and I saw him again later at the market. I don't know anything about him but he just looked shifty. I bet he could be the thief."

"Maybe you're right. I'd say we're gonna find out soon. But for now, let's quiet down and keep our ears open," Bruce whispered.

Lois brushed her hand across the rose pattern embossed into the armchair as she sank into it. Now all she had to do was concentrate on staying awake. Maybe she shouldn't have had such a big supper and cake too. She listened to intermittent creaks as the pine floors cooled after the heat of the day, jumping at each crackle as if it were a pistol shot. Between the creaks, silence filled the room. She didn't know how she would be able to tell whether Bruce and Marge were still awake as she couldn't even hear their breathing.

As Lois listened for any sound in the house, she mentally reviewed everything that had happened since she arrived in Fenwater barely a month ago. So far, her semi-retirement hadn't been as uneventful as she had planned but she was happy here. As she remembered how they had hunted for the watch thief, her head slowly dipped toward her chest. In her mind she was re-living the closing cere-mony of the sesquicentennial week, where she and Marge were lauded for capturing the thief, when a noise in the kitchen wakened her. She didn't know how long she had dozed but it was still dark. To make it easier to gain entry to the house, she hadn't locked the back door. She hoped that the soft rustle from the matching armchair opposite her meant that Marge was awake and had heard the sound too. She strained to catch any sound near the door where Bruce's chair was set but heard nothing.

Several creaks at regular intervals left her in no doubt

that someone was crossing her kitchen and heading toward the dining room. She rose from her chair and waited until she heard the footsteps enter the dining room before she moved to the door leading into the front hall. She stood and listened for more than a minute but the creaking had stopped. Taking a deep breath, she tried to gather the courage to check what was happening in the dining room. She tensed to move, but felt a pair of hands rest on her shoulders and grip her. Stifling a gasp, she relaxed as she realised it must be Bruce behind her. Silently he moved her to one side and tiptoed past her to cross the hallway.

Lois followed Bruce into the dining room. A sliver of light from the curtain she hadn't fully closed allowed her to see a black form standing in front of the sideboard. As she watched, Bruce lunged at the man but the intruder fell a fraction of a second before her friend could grab him. As the intruder clattered to the floor, the chandelier hanging over the dining room table twinkled to life. From the corner of her eye, Lois saw Marge standing in the doorway at the light switch.

The man on the floor groaned, rubbing his shoulder. "What kind of woman tackles like that?"

Lois stifled a laugh as she noticed the grey form hovering behind the prone intruder. Beldie, her resident ghost and protector, was becoming less solid, fading away now that its work was done. She nodded her thanks to the ghostly animal. The goat's intelligent, wide-set eyes seemed to acknowledge her gratitude before it disappeared completely.

The man remained on the floor, staring up at Bruce. "Oh, it was you that hit me. Might have known that wasn't a woman."

"Norm! You're the last person I expected," Bruce replied. "But I didn't touch you. You must have tripped."

Lois stayed silent. She didn't intend to tell them that a ghost had tackled the man. Since no one else seemed to be able to see Beldie except her, she doubted they would believe her.

Bruce reached down and pulled the other man to his feet then manoeuvred him into a chair at the dining room table. He positioned himself in front of Norm to prevent him from escaping and said over his shoulder, "Marge, will you call the police?"

"Oh, come on, Bruce. You don't need to do that – we can sort this out ourselves," Norm said, his voice strained.

"I don't think so. You put Greg in hospital and were cool as a cucumber at the market when you told us about it only a short while later. And you stole from Dave. We've known you for years – well, I thought I knew you," Bruce said.

"So it was you that broke into Greg's house," Lois said. "And that was your second time at the market that day when we met you. You must have timed a morning trip to the market to be there when Dave was across the road at the Honey Pot."

Norm rubbed his shoulder as he nodded. "Yeah, that's right. I knew he and Roy meet up for coffee on Saturdays."

"Why?" Bruce asked. "You're not short of money."

"No, that's true. But I've got one of the best Native art collections in the province. That rare bowl would've been the pièce de résistance – if I could just have found out who bought it. I was outbid for it at the auction and I've been trying to find out who bought it ever since. The auction house wouldn't tell me and they said the buyer wouldn't consider any offers for it either. So I started targeting anyone I heard about that had Haida carvings. I figured I would eventually find the piece I was after."

"There's where you made a mistake. You should have

left the wrong bowls with their owners so no one would figure out what you were looking for," Lois said.

Norm nodded wearily. "Yeah. Guess I was greedy. The other carvings aren't worth as much as the grease bowl but they are valuable and made nice additions to my collection."

Lois glared at the intruder. "And you'd hurt your friends to get them. How could you even think about doing that? Well, I'm glad your plan hasn't turned out as well as you hoped."

"No kidding," Norm muttered to himself.

Lois glanced at the clock on the wall and stifled a yawn. It was almost four thirty in the morning and dawn wasn't too far away. She hoped the police wouldn't spend too long taking their statements. She was glad that her plan tonight had worked. All she wanted to do now was fall into her bed. Tomorrow she had no plans to go any further than her veranda all day. She wouldn't tolerate any interruptions. She had a date with a book.

But maybe the day after that she would invite Marge and Bruce around for coffee and they would finish the rest of that spiced apple rum cake.

If you enjoyed *A Craving for Carvings*, won't you please consider leaving a review on Amazon, Goodreads, or any other review site you enjoy? Reviews help readers find new books and consequently benefit authors and readers.

NEWSLETTER

To learn about the latest stories and novels in the *Century Cottage Cozy Mysteries* series, and the author's other books, please sign up to receive **Dianne Ascroft's newsletter**: https://landing.mailerlite.com/webforms/landing/y1k5c3

All information supplied will be kept private and will not be shared.

OTHER TITLES BY THE AUTHOR

A Timeless Celebration
A Century Cottage Cozy Mystery Book 1

When an artefact from the Titanic is stolen before her town's 150th anniversary celebration, it's up to Lois Stone to catch the thief.

Middle-aged widow Lois has moved from bustling Toronto to tranquil Fenwater and is settling into her new life, feeling secure away from the dangers of the city. Then three events happen that shatter her serenity: her house is burgled twice and an antique watch belonging to a Titanic survivor is stolen from the local museum. Her best friend, Marge was responsible for the watch's safekeeping until its official presentation to the museum at the town's 150th anniversary party and its disappearance will jeopardise her job. Lois won't let her friend's reputation be tarnished or her job endangered by an accusation of theft. She's determined to find the watch in time to save her best friend's job and the town's 150th anniversary celebration.

And so begins a week of new friends, apple and cinnamon muffins, calico cats, midnight intruders, shadowy caprine companions and more than one person with a reason to steal the watch, set against the backdrop of century houses on leafy residential streets, the swirling melodies of bagpipes, a shimmering heat haze and the burble of cool water. *A Timeless Celebration* is the story of Lois's unwitting entry into the world of amateur sleuthing in a small town which beckons readers to stop and stay a while.

The novel is available on Amazon in paperback and e-book. For details, visit Dianne's Amazon page:

Amazon US: https://www.amazon.com/Dianne-Ascroft/e/B002BOCBKA

Amazon UK: https://www.amazon.co.uk/Dianne-Ascroft/e/B002BOCBKA

Out of Options
A Century Cottage Cozy Mysteries novella

A dry district, a shocking secret, a missing person.

Middle-aged widow Lois is settling into life on her own in her neighbourhood and in the library where she works, and she is just about coping with her fear of strangers after her husband was mugged and died in the park at the end of their street. But her quiet existence is rocked when her friend and fellow local historical society researcher, Beth, arranges to meet her to reveal an exciting and shocking discovery she has made about the history of prohibition in West Toronto Junction, the last dry area in Toronto, and then goes missing before she can share her secret with Lois. There isn't any proof that Beth is missing so the police won't actively search for her. Only Lois and Beth's niece

Amy are convinced that Beth's disappearance is very out of character, and they are worried about her. Where has Beth gone? Is she in danger? And, if she is, who might want to harm her and why? Lois knows she must find the answers to these questions fast if she wants to help and protect her friend.

And so begins a weekend of skulking in the park, apple and cinnamon pancakes, familiar faces staring out of old newspapers, calico cats, shadows on the windowpane, and more than one person who might want Beth to disappear from the quiet, leafy streets of the historic and staunchly dry West Toronto Junction neighbourhood.

The novella is available on Amazon in paperback and e-book. For details, visit Dianne's Amazon page:

Amazon **US:** https://www.amazon.com/Dianne-Ascroft/e/B002BOCBKA

Amazon **UK:** https://www.amazon.co.uk/Dianne-Ascroft/e/B002BOCBKA

ABOUT THE AUTHOR

Dianne Ascroft is a Canadian who has settled in rural Northern Ireland. She and her husband live on a small farm with an assortment of strong-willed animals.

She is currently writing the Century Cottage Cozy Mysteries series. *A Craving for Carvings* is a short story in the series.

Her previous fiction works include *The Yankee Years* series of novels and short reads, set in Northern Ireland during the Second World War; *An Unbidden Visitor* (a tale inspired by Fermanagh's famous Coonian ghost); *Dancing Shadows, Tramping Hooves: A Collection of Short Stories* (contemporary tales), and an historical novel, *Hitler and Mars Bars*, which explores Operation Shamrock, a little known Irish Red Cross humanitarian endeavour.

Dianne writes both fiction and non-fiction. Her articles and short stories have been printed in Canadian and Irish magazines and newspapers.

For more information about the author and her books, visit

her website: www.dianneascroft.com
her Facebook page: www.facebook.com/DianneAscroftwriter
Twitter: @DianneAscroft
Sign up for her newsletter: landing.mailerlite.com/webforms/landing/y1k5c3

Made in the USA
Coppell, TX
22 November 2024

40808240R00021